D0574141

It's Valentine's Day, Chloe Zoe!

Jane Smith

Albert Whitman & Company
Chicago, Illinois

It's Valentine's Day!

Valentine's Day is for sharing lots of love with your family and friends.

There are so many ways to say "I love you!"

Last year Mommy and Daddy gave me lots of chocolate hearts.

I made fancy paper flowers for Mommy,

a heart wand for my little sister,
and cupcakes for Daddy. Yum!

This year, my class is having a valentine exchange.
Everyone made shoebox mailboxes in arts and crafts.

I have Princess Kitty valentines for my class. Plus I made an extra-special valentine for each of my extra-special friends.

My mommy helped me cut out white, pink, and red paper hearts. I fancied them up with buttons, lace, glitter, and candy. I used lots and lots of glue!

I drew everyone's favorite things on the valentines for my extra-special friends: red roses for Teacher Amy, everything pink, pink, pink for Mary Margaret, and a red robot plus a cherry lollipop for George.

Beep
Boop

Then I carefully packed them up into my backpack. I didn't want any of my valentines to get squished!

At school, I was excited to see Mary Margaret's bright pink valentines and George's crazy-cupid-superhero valentines. I told them mine were going to be a surprise!

George was first walking around the circle, placing a valentine in each mailbox along the way.

Leo was next. Then Ben, followed by the twins, Violet and Vivian, and Mary Margaret.

When it was my turn, I pranced around the circle, giving out all my valentines. But when I got to George, I reached into my bag for the red-robot-lollipop valentine and the bag was EMPTY!

My belly did a flip-flop. I was so careful packing up all the valentines. Where could it be? What if it was lost forever?

A couple tears welled up and Teacher Amy came over.

"What's wrong, Chloe Zoe?" she asked.

"My special valentine for George is gone!" I sniffed.

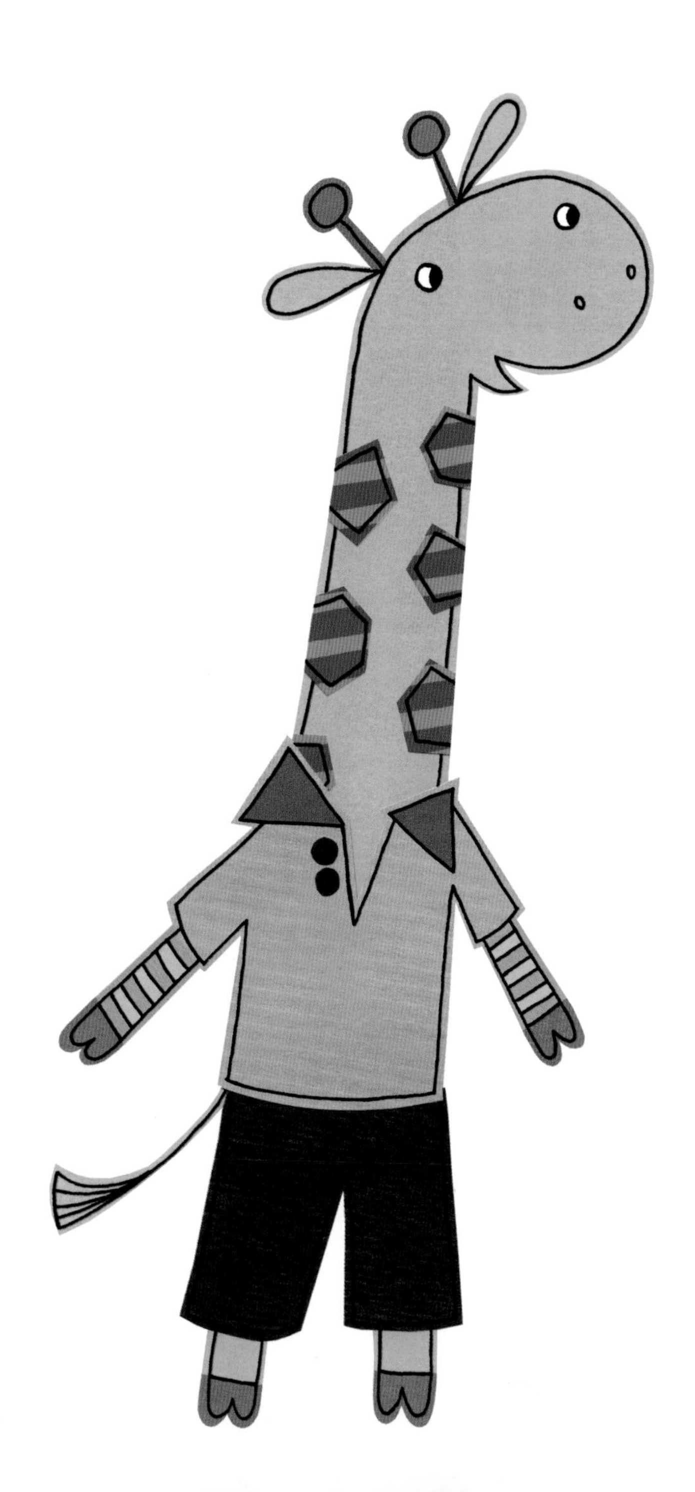

“Maybe it just fell out of your bag,” suggested Teacher Amy. “Let’s go look around.”

Mary Margaret grabbed my hand. “Don’t worry, Chloe Zoe,” she said. “We’ll find it.”

Everyone spread out to search the room. We looked under chairs, over the tabletops, across the floor, and inside the cubbies.

ABC......

ABC......

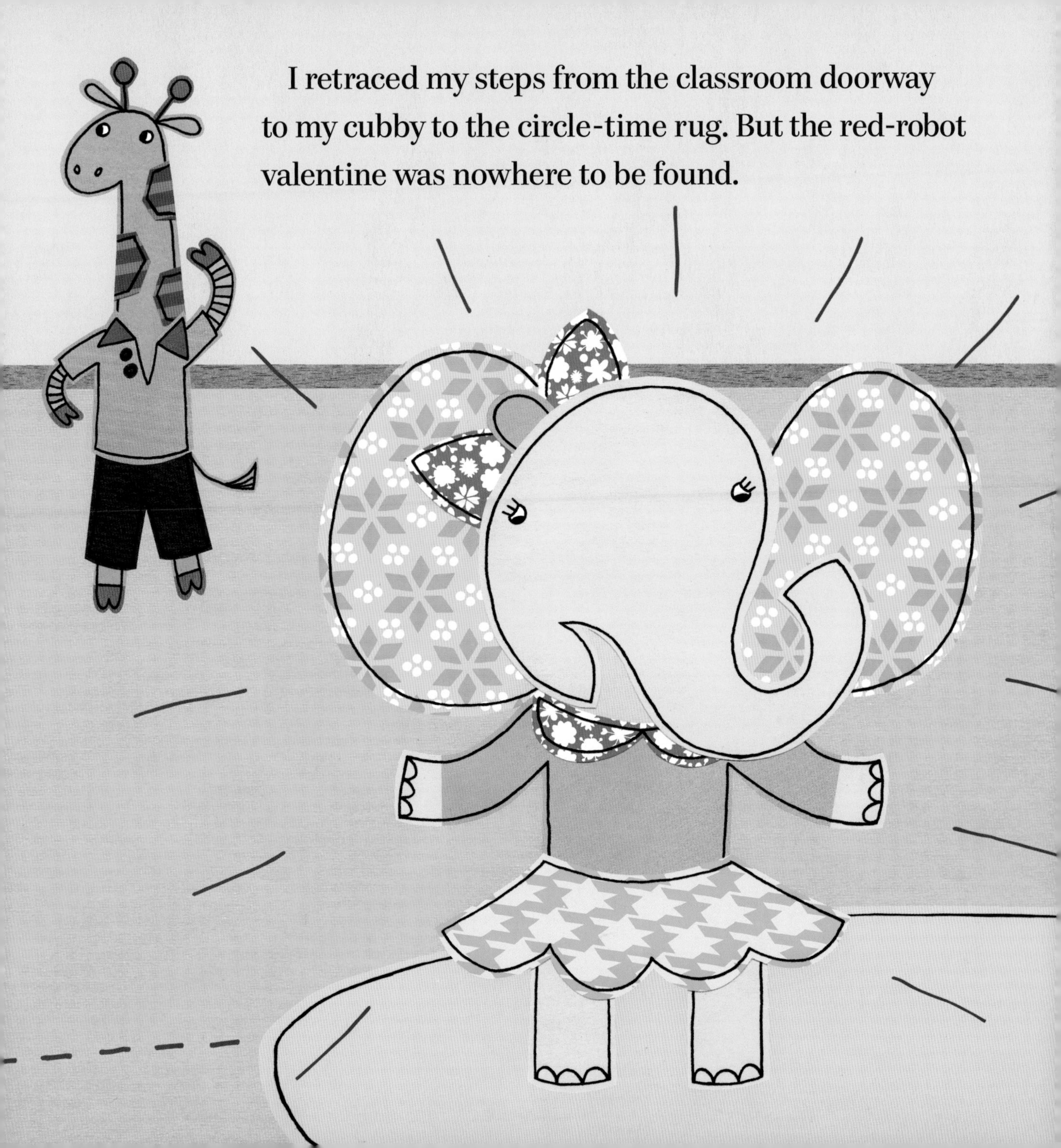

I retraced my steps from the classroom doorway to my cubby to the circle-time rug. But the red-robot valentine was nowhere to be found.

“I’m so sorry, George,” I said.

“It’s OK, Chloe Zoe,” George said. “You and Mary Margaret are my best friends. I know that even without a special valentine.”

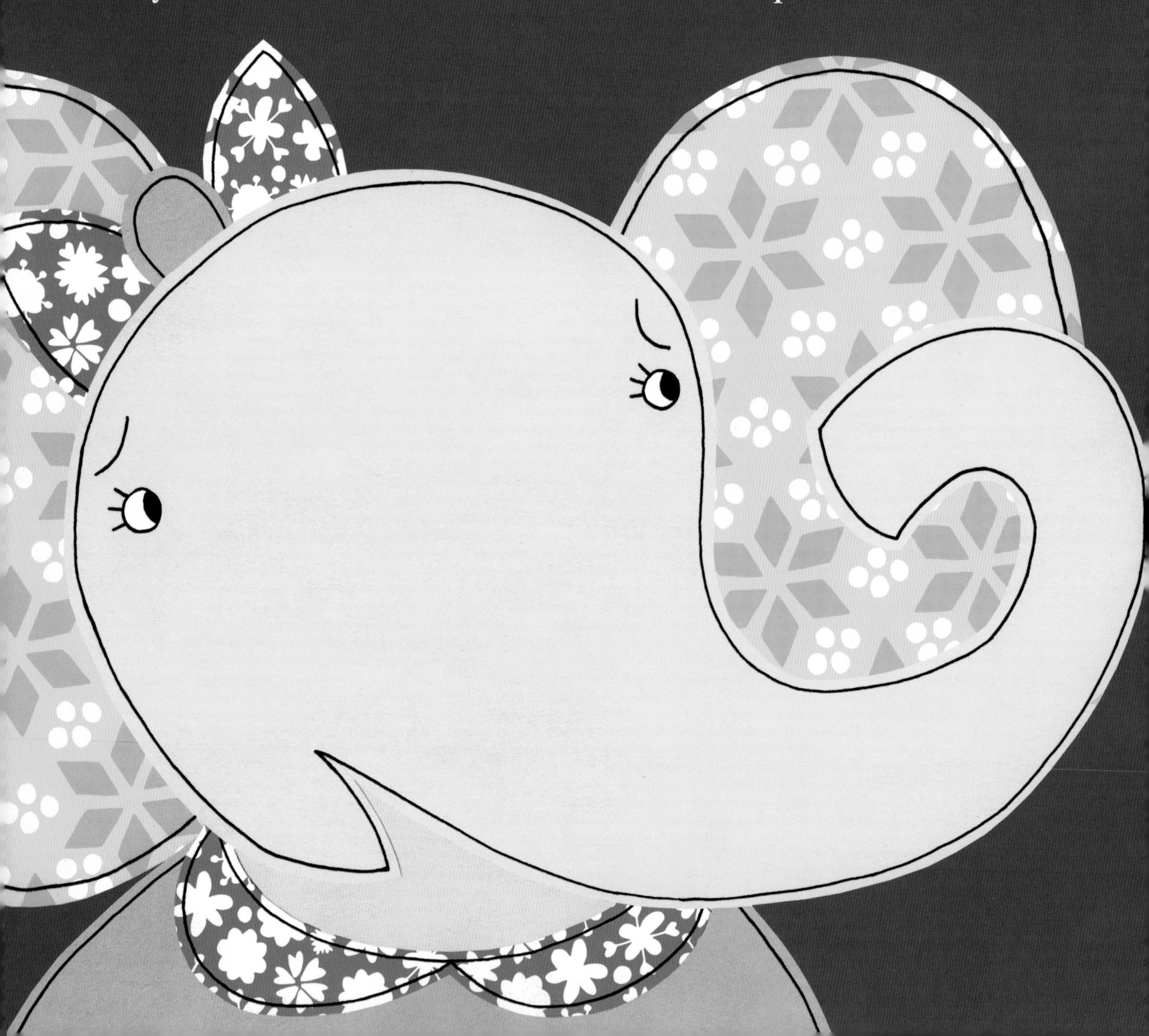

Just then, Mary Margaret came running over. She was holding up my backpack. The red-robot valentine was stuck to the bottom of it.

"Look! I found It!"

My heart skipped a beat! Carefully, I separated a blob of dried glue on the valentine from my backpack. With a big smile, I finally presented my special valentine to George.

“Happy Valentine’s Day, Chloe Zoe!” shouted George. And all my friends cheered!

For more Chloe Zoe fun
—like crafts, coloring pages, games, and activities—
visit www.albertwhitman.com.

For Chris, who has never stopped
believing in me XOXO!

Also available:
It's Easter, Chloe Zoe!

More Chloe Zoe books coming soon:
It's the First Day of Preschool, Chloe Zoe!
It's the First Day of Kindergarten, Chloe Zoe!

Library of Congress Cataloging-in-Publication data is on file with the publisher.

Published in 2016 by Albert Whitman & Company
ISBN 978-0-8075-2462-6

Printed in China
10 9 8 7 6 5 4 3 2 1 HH 24 23 22 21 20 19 18 17 16 15

Design by Jordan Kost

For more information about Albert Whitman & Company, visit our web site at www.albertwhitman.com.